Snowman's Secret

by Robert Barry
pictures by Edward Frascino

MACMILLAN PUBLISHING CO., INC.
New York
COLLIER MACMILLAN PUBLISHERS
London

Macmillan Publishing Co., Inc.,
866 Third Avenue, New York, N.Y. 10022
Collier Macmillan Canada, Ltd.

Printed in the United States of America

1 2 3 4 5 6 7 8 9 10

Library of Congress Cataloging in Publication Data
Barry, Robert E   Snowman's secret.
[1. Snow—Fiction] I. Frascino, Edward.
II. Title.   PZ7.B2804Sn   [E]   75-15801   ISBN 0-02-708390-X

For My Mother and Father

Billy, Jennifer, Susan, Peter, Wendy and
Ebeneezer built an enormous snowman.

He was a very special snowman.
He had a secret.

After a while, the snowman started to melt.
He lost his grin.

Icicles dripped slowly from his chin
and hung down in whiskers.
He turned into an old man with a cane.
But that was not the secret.

The old man's buttons popped off one by one,
and he began to collapse.

Now he looked like a circus elephant.
His trunk stuck fast to a mound of snow.
But that was not the secret.

Then the elephant started to crack.
Billy and Jennifer built him up into a mighty fortress.

Peter and Susan battered the fortress to smithereens.

Ebeneezer howled and ate some of it.

But that was not the secret.

Wendy plowed through the ruins on her sled...
THUD!

And the ruins became a giant pair of ice skates.
But that was not the secret.

The skates dissolved, bit by bit, and there stood
a reindeer with sparkling antlers.

Drip by drip, the reindeer turned into
a rabbit huddled in the snow.
But that was not the secret.

The rabbit tumbled down and melted and melted...
into a mouse.
Billy, Jennifer, Susan, Peter, Wendy and Ebeneezer
were watching when the mouse just faded away.
Then they discovered the snowman's secret.

And right in the middle, where the snow mouse
had disappeared, was Ebeneezer's bright blue collar!